Little Lou and the Woolly Mammoth

PAULA BOWLES

BLOOMSBURY

LONDON NEW DELHI NEW YORK SYDNEY

Being a curious kind of a girl,
Little Lou decided to give it a tug.

But the thread wriggled away! So she followed it instead.

It wound around and around,

it looped up and down

and it twisted

and tangled in

lots of knots.

Little Lou followed the thread overhead and
around the bend, until finally it ended in a

monstrous, tangled mess!

But what could it be?

"Wait! Come back!" called Little Lou.

And they zigged and they zagged

until they could zigzag no more.

And the poor woolly mammoth trembled and shook as
Little Lou bent down and picked him up from the floor.
And gave him . . .